QUEEN OF THE PEN BOOKS™
Published by Queen of the Pen Books™
Queen of the Pen Books™ USA
P.O. Box 68221, Schaumburg, Illinois 60168, USA

Copyright © 2010-2013 by Clarissa Burton

This book is a piece of fiction. Names, characters, and incidents are the products of the author's imagination or used fictitiously. Any resemblance to actual events, locales, or persons living or dead is purely coincidental.

All rights reserved.

No part of this book may be reproduced, stored in a retrieval system, or transmitted by any manner without permission of the author. Please do not participate in or encourage piracy of copyrighted materials in violation of the author's rights. Purchase only authorized editions.

ISBN-13: 978-0615847054
ISBN-10: 0615847056

Faces ~ Samantha

A NOVEL BY
Clarissa Burton

Acknowledgement

I never know from where my inspiration for a story will come. This book is one of a series of stories that have lain dormant within me for decades. It took the reading of the story of a real little girl going through pain and suffering that inspired the release of this first book.

For all those little girls who are going through such horrific pain and suffering, I write this for you.

For all women who are trapped in the essence of a little girl and fighting to get past the hurt and suffering of abuse, I write this story for you.

For the love of my life, J, I write this series for you because it is because of your love that I am able to tell this story.

For my children and grandchildren, my love for you got me through the darkest days.

For my dear friends, especially the Elite 5, you continually encourage and support my love of writing. I write for you, too.

Finally, I send love and great appreciation to

my sister, Veloria Sims-James. You have been there for me even when distance and years stood between us. Your editing talents have saved the day many times. Thank you for keeping it honest and forthright. We are going to make this happen big! - Love your big sis!

Author's Insight

I have always known that everyone had a story to tell. Whether true or fictional, it is the stories of those who dare to put their soul to pen and paper that allows the universe to thrive. My life is full of such stories, some good and a lot bad. Sanity lies between our choice to either wallow in self-pity or take those life experiences and molding them into a work of art that touches someone's life.

Faces ~ Samantha is that type of story. The first *Faces* novel series that tells the story of eight-year-old Samantha Roberts and her struggle to be a child in an adult world. She faces a self-imposed responsibility from keeping her brother safe from harm, her attempts to reassemble her parents' broken relationship, to demanding her right to be a child. Unfortunately, many children can relate to Samantha's plight and they, too, carry these burdens into adulthood. Some may recover and move on to a fulfilled life, while others will remain eight-years old emotionally and psychologically.

The characters in this novel series could be any one of us. Their agony, betrayals, disappointments, hurts, struggles, and triumphs are ours as well. No one escapes the sorrows and joys of others. We sometimes turn our heads and pretend the universe belongs to the individual. However, life is amazing. It often blindsides us, reminding us that we are not islands.

So as you read this novel, search for a part of yourself in each character. Of course, you will be uncomfortable; but the beginning of healing is recognizing you are human and are allowed to feel pain, growing pains. You will not find a character that matches you exactly; but there is a part of each of us in each of them.

Grow with Samantha, Tavis, Tanya, and Grayson. Thank you for reading.

Clarissa

Prologue

The Curio

Journal Entry-May 27, 1989

My life has been a colorful and emotional journey. I don't know when I matured enough to recognize what had happened to me at eight-years old, and how different I would be at twenty-three. Yet, tortured memories of my childhood have enslaved me. My relationship with my parents has begun to recover, especially my relationship with my mother.

Often I want to disappear into another world, where I would remain untouched, undamaged.

However, I am still here sitting in my beautifully, decorated studio apartment, a constant reminder of Mom, our tenuous relationship, her need for independence, and my need for her acceptance.

Mom imprinted my apartment with her decorating style. Don't get me wrong, everything is beautiful and very expensive. She spared no expense. From the Lebanese hand-woven, black and gold living room rug, to the caramel accent walls, they sing my mother's praises. Every original oil painting and Japanese porcelain Saki cup, pose for her spirit. As lovely as my apartment is, I feel no spiritual connection, except for the photo I took of Tavis and me during our European tour last year, which sits on the top shelf of the Curio.

Of course, she' my mother; but I don't know how or why we have become emotional and psychological leeches in each other's worlds. My only consolation and freedom lies within the mahogany, glass-framed curio. Upon those shelves my soul lives. I regularly visit it, rearranging and dusting its delicate onyx crystal, residents, the little girl figurines. I don't recall exactly when I became fascinated, even obsessed, with the figurines. One day while window-shopping at the local mall, I noticed these beautiful, handcrafted black, glimmering, crystal beauties. They beckoned me and I had to have them. My therapist explained they represent my attempt to control my emotional turmoil. She also said my obsessive, compulsive cleaning and constant rearranging of the figurines represent my desire to clean off the 'dirty' of my past. Additionally, their delicate beauty reassured the lost girl she was also fragile, and beautiful.

When I pick up an onyx crystal figurine, I hold it gently, but firmly in my hands to ensure I do no harm. With a soft, thin microfiber washrag, I gently caress each gleaming statuette ensuring not to cause the slightest damage. I don't want to ruin the crystal beauties. They are fragile like me. I have seen and felt more pain than any child should. I'm still fragile.

Today, I followed the same cleaning routine. As

I had returned the last of the delicate nymphs to her safe cradle, and secure them behind the safety of the curio doors, when I noticed the *Girl* again. She stared through me with those innocent blue, empty eyes. The *Girl* haunts me day and night, reminding me of a stolen childhood and an adulthood stalked by the past. I try to convince her to let it go, that I want to move on. I remind her that at least I'm still here, that maybe I can be fixed.

She doesn't believe me. Standing silently from beyond the curio's wonderland, I feel her desire for spiritual freedom. Her spirit beckons me to return to that cold, wet winter's morning when the *Girl* laid between life and death. My eyes pleaded with her to leave me alone. I wanted freedom from that painful past that rests upon my soul slowly picking away at its life. As usual, she refuses. Determined to keep my soul hostage and pull it back to the bitterly frozen asphalt outside General Hospital, I surrendered. What's weird is, the beautiful, blue-eyed doppelganger isn't forceful. She's always gentle yet uncompromising.

Did I hear her whisper a familiar name? Yes, she had. Through unmoving lips, I heard her say, *"Tavvy needs you complete. You must to go back to where it all began."*

Fear struck me deeply. Why the urgency? I adored my baby brother. Tavvy has always been a good kid; but lately something had changed. Our childhood experiences left deep emotional wounds. I feared he would never recover. However, as time passed, Tavis appeared to be all right. He excelled academically and athletically. He even interned with Daddy at the law firm. However, lately I've noticed a change in Tavis. Outwardly, he laughed, smiled, and seemed happy. However, he and I had a special connection, and now, he's quite different. Our connection is broken.

After my hospitalization at General Hospital, all I wanted was to return to the life Tavvy and I had known, a life with our daddy feeding mallards and geese at the neighborhood park, beautiful Mill Creek

Park. Although we did return home and to feeding our favorite birds, life wasn't the same.

The girl continued to beckon me. There was no escape. Determined to take my soul hostage until I finished what life had begun, I surrendered. I didn't know how or where to begin, or if I was emotionally and psychologically strong enough to finish. My insecurities were irrelevant.

As I looked closer, I noticed her face was wet with blood-soaked tears. Suddenly, I was flooded with the horrific memories of that cold, wintery morning, when the *Girl* was thrown from the dented, green 1980 Buick Pontiac station wagon, onto the wet, cold asphalt near the Hospital's emergency room. She had won. Realizing this was also for Tavis, with shaking hands, I reached for her ghostly, extended hand, and we returned to that dark, frigid day.

Now, I remember . . .

Part I
Samantha

Chapter One

A Day to Remember

Samantha looked at the *Girl* in the mirror wondering what was wrong with her.

"You nasty, stupid little girl!" she screamed at the scared reflection. "So very ugly."

This was far from the truth. Samantha was a lovely, caramel-skinned girl with a perfect button nose and a smile that lit up every room she entered. She had jet black, wavy, shoulder length hair and beautiful blue eyes like her little brother, Tavis. They inherited their beautiful blue eyes from their father,

Grayson. Inheriting their father's features seemed to make their mother, Tanya, dislike her and Tavis more. It didn't matter that Samantha was a duplicate image of her mother, Tanya didn't show interest nor affection toward her children. It didn't matter how pretty she was, Samantha's self-image and confidence were nothing. If her mother never told her she was pretty or lovable, then it must be true that Samantha was ugly and unlovable.

When she confronted the ugliness in the mirror, all Samantha could think about was how she felt unloved by her mother, and abused by her babysitter, and the sitter's sons. For Samantha, mean things only happened to ugly, little girls. That was her way of justifying her abusers' behavior. She believed when someone is lovable, people treated them like gold by giving praise, encouragement, love and affection. The only person who showed the kids love was their father, grandparents, and Aunt Carol. However, their father was gone and their grandparents and aunt weren't around.

Still staring at the image in the mirror, Samantha hated and pitied the Girl more. She began to think that maybe her father didn't love her after all.

"Who could blame him for leaving? Who could love an ugly and dirty girl?" She asked the wounded girl who blankly gazed back at her.

fffff

That day was supposed to be Samantha's and Tavis' last day at Ms. Essie's house. It would be the very last time they would set foot in that dreary, torturous place; but not before knocking at death's door. As the darkness crept upon the afternoon, there was no word from their mother. Samantha's mother had threatened her and Tavis that this would be the last day they would see her for the rest of their lives. Lately, Tanya often threatened to return them to their father. She told them they had become too much of an emotional and financial burden. She wanted her freedom and realized taking the children from Grayson was a big mistake.

It didn't matter what her mother's reasons

were, all Samantha could think about was never seeing that fat, horrible Ms. Essie again. She and Tavis would finally be rid of their babysitter's brutal beatings, the sexual abuse from her sadistic sons, and being forced to eat cold, boll weevil infested oatmeal. Finally, she could ask her father why he had abandoned them.

fffff

Each morning when Tanya dropped Samantha and Tavis off at Ms. Essie's, she would send a grocery bag containing breakfast cereal, milk, and snacks for after school, food the children were rarely fed. Ms. Essie would greet Tanya with a big smile and her nauseating religious greeting, "God bless you, Tanya. Praise be to God."

Samantha couldn't understand why her mother couldn't see through Ms. Essie's fakeness. She was such an evil woman. Samantha made many attempts to tell Tanya how Ms. Essie and her sons treated Tavis and her. However, Tanya refused to listen or she would defend Ms. Essie.

One day after Tanya had picked Samantha and Tavis up, she noticed Samantha sniffling. "What's your problem?" Tanya asked, glaring at Samantha in the rear-view mirror.

"Nothing," Samantha lied, trying to control her tears.

"Don't lie to me. What's your problem? You had better tell me or I'll smack you when we get home."

Taking a deep breath and fearing her mother's wrath, Samantha began to share what had happened to Tavis at Ms. Essie's house.

"Ms. Essie's sons, Mark and James, put a belt around Tavvy's neck and hung him from a hook on the back porch," Samantha said between sobs. The more she thought about what had happened to Tavis, the deeper her sobs.

Samantha looked up at her mother. She wanted to see if Tanya would be angry enough to protect her children and refuse to take them back to Ms. Essie's. She thought surely this monstrous act would spark righteous anger from her mother toward Ms. Essie and her lynch mob, maybe get revenge.

Tanya pulled the car over and stopped. She allowed the car to idle for several minutes and continued to glare at Samantha through the rear-view mirror. After a few minutes of angry silence, Tanya turned around looking Samantha in the eyes. The anger Samantha saw in her mother's eyes wasn't for Ms. Essie. It was for her.

"What did you just say?" Tanya asked.

"Mark and James put a belt around Tavvy's neck and hung him!" Samantha repeated tearfully.

In an instant, Samantha's face jerked to the left hitting against the rear, passenger window. The sting engulfed her entire body. Tanya had slapped her! Trying to grasp what had just happened, Samantha heard her mother scream at her.

"How dare you say such horrible things about that Christian woman and her family? That woman has been like a godly grandmother to you and Tavis," Tanya bellowed angrily. "Ms. Essie didn't have to babysit for me. I had to beg her because I needed to work to support us. Now, you're making up lies about her! I know why you're doing this. You want to go back to your father. I won't allow it. You're just a trouble maker and a liar!"

"I'm not lying, Mom! Look at Tavvy's neck. It's black and blue."

Ignoring Samantha's story and refusing to look at Tavis' injuries, Tanya quickly turned around toward the steering wheel, put the car into drive, and headed their secret shelter. She refused to check Tavis' neck. Tanya was terrified. Her vengeful plans were beginning to unravel. She began to panic because legal authorities might charge her with child abuse and neglect. Tanya didn't want to believe Samantha because if she was telling the truth, she would have to admit she had failed as a mother and leaving Grayson was a bad idea.

"This is why I didn't want kids. They are too much trouble. Grayson, this is entirely your fault!" Tanya cursed under her breath.

Samantha turned to look at Tavis and at his swollen neck. He was crying. Samantha felt helpless. She reached for his hand and held it tightly. Silently, with her eyes she reassured him she would do whatever it took to keep him safe from that day forward.

fffff

At eight years old, Samantha had grown up quickly. She and her four year old little brother, Tavis, lived with their mother, Tanya, who was estranged from their father, and told her children their father, Grayson , left his family for a woman with six children. Tanya was very bitter for having children. She was pretty, smart, and a very talented clothing designer. Yet, she took out her frustrations on Samantha and Tavis.

Her negative behavior toward her children confused Tanya, too. She never had a childhood because Tanya's parents made her take care of their babies. The only freedom she had to be a kid was when she was in school. When she became a mother,

Tanya didn't know how to love a child. She knew how to change diapers and wipe dirty noses; but having motherly instincts were foreign. Now, she faced two little people who were depending on her to protect them. Tanya was emotionally lost.

fffff

Samantha was responsible for cooking, cleaning, and getting herself ready for school and Tavis ready for daycare. Although they lived twenty minutes from Ms. Essie's, Tanya often demanded Samantha walk her little brother to the babysitter's house before school. It didn't matter if there was several feet of snow or ice-slicked sidewalks; and the tortuous journey usually took at least an hour. Rain, sleet, or snow wouldn't change her mother's mind.

"I don't have time for all this shit. I never wanted you! I didn't ask to be left with you two. Your daddy didn't want you, and now I'm stuck with you. You need to get your brother to the babysitter's before you go to school; and I don't care how you do it. Just get him there, you hear me?" Tanya hissed through clenched teeth.

"Yes, Ma'am," Samantha replied, her heart stinging from her mother's bitter and poisonous words. She hoped her mother wouldn't kick her this time.

Tanya had never hit her children before; but since leaving their father, she had begun physically abusing Samantha often. Some angry animal had been unleashed, and Tanya was out of control.

There would be no reprieve for Samantha this morning. Tanya pretended to walk away, but quickly turned and drop kicked Samantha in the stomach. Samantha screamed out grabbing her stomach and toppled to the floor. She quickly put her hand to her mouth knowing that if she hadn't, her mother would follow up with more kicks and punches.

"Now, get your stupid ass up, get you and your brother dressed, and get out of my damn house!"

fffff

As Samantha and Tavis disappeared into their room, Tanya walked over to the kitchen sink and threw up. She couldn't believe what a monster she had become. Why did she hurt Samantha? Although her parents weren't the best and left her to take care of her brothers and sisters, they never physically harmed their children. Where was this anger coming from? Tanya threw up again. She turned on the faucet, watching her nervous guilt washing down the drain.

Taking a wet dishcloth, Tanya wiped her mouth and headed toward the kids' room. Putting her ear to the door, she could hear Samantha crying and Tavis trying to comfort her.

"God, I must get help. I'm out of control!" For the first time in her life, Tanya felt sadness. She wanted to open the door and beg Samantha's forgiveness; but shame kept her from it.

fffff

Samantha's stomach ached badly. Barely standing upright; Samantha knew she had to get Tavis to the babysitter's house. She had done it before, walking through the pain in her legs, back, and now, her stomach. She was on autopilot. This was typical for Samantha. Luckily, she had been successful at shielding Tavis from their mother's abuse. Samantha knew his little body probably couldn't handle such beatings. If it meant she had to take her mother's physical wrath to save her baby brother, then so be it.

With an achy body and feeling nauseous, Samantha moved very slowly that cold, Midwestern morning. The journey to Ms. Essie's would be very difficult. Regardless, she had to dress Tavis. If she took too long, they would be late leaving, and she would most likely get another beating from their mother.

Tavis wasn't used to the life they were now living. His big sister seemed more tired than usual. He watched Samantha rub her stomach.

"Sammie, you okay?" Tavis asked.

"Yeah, I'm okay, Tavvy," Samantha replied, wincing from a sharp pain in her belly.

"You sure? Then why are you rubbing your

belly? Are you sick again?" Tavis asked, not believing Samantha.

"I'm fine. Get dressed. We have to go."

fffff

At four years old, Tavis had seen more than any child should see. Although Tanya had not put her hands on him, he did everything possible to stay out of her way. He watched in horror as his mother kicked and slapped his big sister. He couldn't understand his mother's abuse toward his sister because Samantha was such a good sister. She always took care of him and did everything their mother asked.

He wanted to protect his Samantha but he was so little. Tavis was very small for a four year old at twenty pounds and standing less than thirty-six inches. He had been born prematurely and his growth was slow. He was the smallest child at the babysitter's house, constantly teased by the bigger kids, especially by Ms. Essie's teenaged sons, who would toss him back and forth like a basketball. They

were so mean and always hurt his big sister. Yet,
Samantha wouldn't talk about it. She would just
wrap her arms around Tavis and tell him how she
would someday get them away from all that
meanness. Tavis loved his big sister so much; but was
very sad he couldn't help her be safe.

Ms. Essie treated the other nicely children who
attended her home daycare. She only treated Tavis
and Samantha badly. It all began when Ms. Essie
discovered they were biracial. She made it known she
hated white people. Often she told Tavis and
Samantha how evil their mother was for breeding
with their father whom she called a white devil and
they were Satan's spawn.

fffff

"Samantha! Get your ass down here and get
that boy to Ms. Essie. I'll beat your ass if you're late.
Now, get out of my damn house!" Tanya hollered
from the bottom of the stairs.

"Come on, Tavvy. We have to go now,"
Samantha said softly, putting Tavis' right arm into his

denim jacket.

"Okay, Sammie. I don't want you hurt no more. I promise to be better next time, okay?" Tavis assured, tears flowing down his chubby cheeks.

"Don't cry, Tavvy. I'm okay," Samantha lied, grabbing Tavis' hand and leading him down the stairs.

"If you're late, Ms. Essie will call me at work; and you will get a beating you will never forget. Do you understand me, girl?" Tanya threatened.

Samantha nodded in acknowledgement as she hurried herself and Tavis into the embrace of winter's coldness. The door slammed behind them, and Samantha and Tavis began their long walk to their torturer's house.

fffff

The school bus dropped Samantha off in front of Ms. Essie's house. Usually, Tavis would wait for her on the front porch. Although it was mid-winter, Ms. Essie made Tavis sit outside for hours. He played alone, pretending his father and Samantha were there

with him. So, when she didn't see him on the front
porch, Samantha became worried. She ran to the
front door and rang the bell. It was always unlocked,
but Samantha knew she had to ring the bell or get a
beating. After ringing the bell twice, Samantha
entered and softly called for Tavis.

"Tavis, where are you?" She called. When there
was no response, panic set in. She continued toward
the kitchen where Ms. Essie always had their snack
bag sitting on the table. They weren't allowed to eat
inside with the other children. She and Tavis had to
eat on the back porch. It was bitterly cold out there;
but at least it was screened in. As she approached the
back porch, Samantha heard moaning and kicking
noises. She also heard laughter. It was Ms. Essie's
sons, Mark and James and several of the other
children.

To her horror, Tavis hung from the back porch
rafters. Mark and James had placed a leather belt
around his tiny neck. Tavis' little hands were
unsuccessfully grasping for space to relieve the

pressure. His lips were blue and his face was turning a deep purple. His little feet were kicking wildly while his torturers and their child minions laughed as if they were watching some comical skit.

Dropping her book bag and shoving Mark and James aside, Samantha jumped on top of the wobbly picnic table under Tavis, and fought to unleash the murderous noose.

"Tavvy please stop kicking! I can't get you down if you keep kicking," Samantha pleaded as his sadistic torturers laughed and taunted.

"Look at that boy jerk. He looks like a fish on a hook," They tormented.

Finally, Samantha was able to unhook the belt loop and she and Tavis fell onto the hard concrete floor. Still laughing, Mark and James herded the other children into the house slamming the backdoor behind them. They left Samantha and Tavis lying on the cold cement floor cradling each other. Hearing their tormenters' evil laughter fade into the walls of the hell house, Samantha sat up and checked Tavis' neck. He was breathing fast and gasping for breath. But, Tavis seemed to be okay. Tavis winced when Samantha touched his bruised neck. Samantha kissed his forehead and wrapped her arms around his shivering body. She removed her coat and covered herself and Tavis.

Samantha inspected Tavis' wounded neck. Blood dripped from the scratches he made trying to loosen the leather noose.

"Ouch!" Tavis' hoarse voice moaned.

"Sorry, Tavvy. After I tell mom what happened, I'm sure she will never bring us back here again," She whispered into Tavis' ear.

Tavis snuggled close to Samantha. After struggling to find a painless position for his head, Tavis finally fell asleep. Snickering continued from their tormenters through the backdoor. As Tavis slept, Samantha yearned for her daddy.

"He would never let this happen to us," She said, watching Tavis sleep and struggle to breath. "I don't think he left us, Tavvy. Daddy loved us too much. It

doesn't make sense. We had too much fun feeding the ducks and geese."

Tavis stirred in his sleep, grimacing as he unconsciously rubbing his sore neck.

It was getting late and the wind blew across their shivering bodies. Ms. Essie only allowed Samantha and Tavis into the house a half-hour before their mother arrived. Samantha was afraid to tell her mother about that day's events. Experience taught her to keep such things to herself. Tanya never believed her kids; and Samantha didn't want to risk punishment. She had to take the chance or Tavis may not make it the next time. Because of Ms. Essie's hatred of their father's whiteness, there would be a next time.

Kissing Tavis on his cheek, Samantha lay down carefully next to him, repositioned her coat, wrapping their bodies like cocooned butterfly larva, and fell asleep.

fffff

The metallic taste was unfamiliar. Blood slowly

oozed out the right side of Samantha's swollen lips. Ms. Essie had hit her hard knocking the tiny girl to the ground, loosening a few teeth in the process.

Nearing one o'clock a.m., the Midwest winter cold engulfed Samantha's beaten and bruised body. As she lay on the cold asphalt, her mind turned to thoughts of Tavis. All she could think about was who would keep her little brother from *the monster*.

"Tavvy, I won't let you down. I will be there to protect you. I promise," she whispered weakly before losing consciousness.

As blood filled her enlarged belly, Samantha faded to black not noticing ER staff rushing to her side. Could they save her? Would she return to protect Tavis from Ms. Essie and her sons? Slipping into the darkness of a coma, Samantha's fight for her and Tavis' lives, had begun.

fffff

It had been two days since Ms. Essie pushed the little girl's body from the car, abandoning her at the hospital. Samantha's body ravaged and bruised with blood dripping between her legs, Ms. Essie knew her sons had gone too far this time. It didn't matter because she was determined to protect them.

"Now, you look here you little hussy! When you get out of this car, I want you to walk inside that door," she instructed, pointing to the emergency room doors.
"Find yourself a doctor, nurse, or anyone. I'm warning you. You had better not tell them the truth. You hear me?" Ms. Essie screamed, poking her sausage-sized index finger into the side of Samantha's forehead.

In shock from the day's sadistic beating and sexual abuse, Samantha sat silently as her consciousness began to fade.

"Did you hear me, wench?" Ms. Essie shouted.

"Yes . . .," Samantha barely whimpered through tears and pain from busted, swollen lips. Her breathing became more shallow and her head ached.

"I-DIDN'T-HEAR-YOU!" Ms. Essie barked.

"Yes," Samantha tried to say louder, but the

abdominal pain was too much.

"Yes, what . . . !" Ms. Essie yelled, pinching the meaty back of Samantha's upper, left arm. It hurt badly but Samantha knew better to cry out or risk more beatings.

"Yes, Ma'am, Ms. Essie," Samantha squeezed out trying to hold back the tears.

"Now, get your sorry ass out of my car; and I better not see your nasty ass again!" Ms. Essie hollered as she pushed Samantha out the passenger door, onto the cold asphalt in front of the General Hospital emergency room.

Landing on her face, Samantha hit the pavement, and heard the screeching bald tires of the wrecked rusty, green 1980 Buick Pontiac station wagon speeding away.

fffff

Trying to keep busy and not think so much about his fragmented family Grayson worked long hours. However, the family photos on his desk and bookshelves betrayed his avoidance. They were constant reminders of his once perfect family life. Grayson wondered if it was all an illusion. Had he focused so much on being the perfect husband, provider, and father that he had missed all the obvious signs of domestic failure? If his parents could be married for nearly thirty years, why couldn't he and Tanya have similar success?

Grabbing his coat, keys, and briefcase, Grayson decided it was time to go home. He was tired; and his office sofa tortured his back. As he descended the office building's stairwell, a sharp pain knocked him to his knees almost causing him to topple down the stairs. Grasping his stomach and breathless, he believed stress had caused ulcers. He quickly sat down to catch his breath. Earlier that month, he had a complete physical and the results were positive. Grayson was as healthy as when he was playing high school football. He couldn't understand the sudden stomach pains that plagued him lately. His family doctor checked for ulcers, appendicitis, and stomach cancer; but all tests returned negative.

As he gathered himself, Grayson shooed it off. He would try to ignore it. However, this pain was different. Meanwhile, the searing pain in Samantha's enlarged stomach intensified.

"Daddy, help me please," She begged. Suddenly, darkness engulfed her.

Chapter Two

Tavvy

Small for his age, Tavis was handsome, and looked like a little doll. Most strangers often mistook Tavis for a toddler and raved about his good looks, especially his handsome, blue eyes. He gloried in the attention, because other than Samantha, no one cared and since their father abandoned them, most of the people in his daily life hurt him. Tavis was glad when people told his big sister she was pretty. That made him happy.

Tavis worshipped his big sister; but the fact that

he could not protect her from the frequent physical and verbal assaults, was torture. He hated Ms. Essie, particularly when she called him "Li'l Man". He knew she hated him and Samantha because she told them often how much she didn't like them and their 'whiteness'. She often rewarded him with long stints in a dark, coat closet. What did a four year old know about being a man? The man who was supposed to be there to groom him left him and his big sister for some woman with six kids.

An angry little boy and confused by his feelings, Tavis knew better than to show it. He just let it bottle up inside. He managed to find one outlet and that was listening to music. Music soothed his deepest anger and tears. The music took him to places his imagination allowed. It temporarily eased the painful life he was living. It was part of his soul and Tavis would sing to Samantha when she was nursing her newest wounds from the day's beatings.

fffff

Ms. Essie was a mean, cruel woman at five-feet,

eleven-inches. She was morbidly obese at about three-hundred eighty pounds. She had a booming voice. The house shook when she walked. Tavis joked to Samantha even the house was afraid of Ms. Essie and that's why it shook so badly. This made Samantha laugh, which Tavis loved. He liked seeing her smile and tried to make her smile as often as possible. He worked hard at being a good boy so Samantha wouldn't get in trouble because of him. Making her laugh was the highlight of his day.

What scared Tavis most were Ms. Essie's teenaged sons, Mark and James. They were bullies and seemed to relish in their hateful talents. They often picked Tavis up, tossing him to each other like a living basketball.

"Here he comes, Mark! Don't miss or we will have a mess on our hands," James chuckled before tossing Tavis.

"Oh. . .Oh. . . Ha! Ha! I almost missed, "Mark said, pretending to almost drop Tavis.

Each time this happened, Tavis would pee his

pants from fright. He thought he could handle it; but the thought of getting thrown and dropped always got the best of him.

"You nasty little bastard! Go clean yourself or else I'll tell mama you pissed your pants. Now, get away from me!" Mark shouted, pushing the crying Tavis to the floor.

Tavis couldn't understand what he had done to deserve such mean treatment. He was a good little boy. He didn't hurt animals or disrespect people. He always said "Yes, Sir", "Yes, Ma'am", and "Thank, you." But no matter how polite, Tavis always seemed to get punished by Ms. Essie's blood thirsty spawn. To ease the pain, Tavis would crawl under the bed in the room Ms. Essie set up for babysitting, which had a radio on all the time. He would lie closest to the radio, close his eyes and listen to the music of Minnie Ripperton, Tina Turner, Elton John, and others. His favorite musician was Stevie Wonder. His music was soothing, kind, and sweet; and Tavis just wanted to live in the words of Stevie's songs. If he could, he would listen to *"Isn't She Lovely"*, all day long. Music was his only escape from the horrors of the Essie torture chamber.

fffff

When Tavis saw Samantha lying next to him on the floor bloody and motionless, he was horrified. He didn't know what to do. All he knew was he had to escape. He was only four-years old. Where would he go? Tavis yearned for the protection of his daddy.

Where was his daddy when he needed him most? *How could Daddy leave us?* Tavis silently asked, unable to understand why his father would abandon him and Samantha, leaving them to be abused by such cruel people. Although his mother had never shown him affection, Tavis still loved her. He was confused. How could she allow such bad things to happen to him and Samantha? Isn't a mother supposed to love her children?

Tavis scooted closer to Samantha and placed his face next to hers. Tears puddles beneath Tavis and Samantha. All he could do was pray someone would rescue them soon.

fffff

The day was hectic. The day for Tanya's well-planned escape had finally arrived. The radical underground organization that helps mothers escape abusive relationships had contacted her with the covert escape procedures. She would take only necessities, thirty-thousand dollars in cash she accumulated in small amounts for over a year as not to tip off Grayson. She obtained passports for herself and the kids just in case they had to leave the country, and kept their departure secret from close friends, extended family, and the kids.

The organization had strict weekly attendance requirements. They made it clear that if one meeting was missed, Tanya would be dropped from their program. She lied that she feared for her life and the lives of her children. Tanya stated she needed assistance getting to safety without her abusive husband's knowledge. The organization would provide a safe haven for her and the kids in a secret community that included a homeschooling system with busing, childcare, and religious services. The program provided detailed outlines for every activity. All participants were to follow the strict outlines as provided if the organization was to remain successful.

The day of departure arrived and Tanya was anxious. Grayson would be out of town for a few days on business. She hadn't considered one particular problem: Grayson's parents. His parents called each right at exactly fifteen minutes before bedtime to speak with the kids. Tanya had to depart promptly at 8:30 p.m., which was when the grandparents usually ended their call. She had to calm herself and act her usual cool self. If she didn't, everyone would suspect something was amidst.

For a moment, Tanya began to question if taking the children from Grayson was a good idea. She could just drop Samantha and Tavis off at the Roberts, take the thirty-thousand and start a new life in another country. That would be the easiest solution to her self-induced misery. However, Tanya's envious side ignored any rational thoughts. She wanted to hurt Grayson and the best way to do so was by taking his most precious loves, Samantha and Tavis. Nevertheless, how would she convince the kids to go with her? Although she was their mother, Tanya had never bonded with Samantha or Tavis. When she attempted to hold or kiss them, the kids' bodies stiffened and sometimes shook. Tanya knew they were afraid of her. Their fear was perfect for her plan. She had an idea, a sinister one. She would write a letter to the kids, telling them it was from their father.

Sitting at Grayson's desk in his home office, Tanya roll a piece of typing paper into the IBM Smith Selectric typewriter. After discarding several drafts, she removed the last draft and read it aloud.

My Darling Samantha and Tavis:

It has taken me a long time to write this letter. What I have to write is so hard. I have tried to be a good daddy to you. I have tried loving you; but I just don't know how. I have decided I don't want to be a daddy anymore. It's too

hard. I hope you can forgive me; but I think
this is for the best. Go with your mother. She
will take better care of you.
Love, Daddy

Tanya sat back in Grayson's leather office chair, sheepishly smiling at her written poison. Satisfied with the final draft, she placed the forgery in an envelope, wrote Samantha's and Tavis' names on it, and quietly placed it on the kitchen counter in front of the coffee maker.

It was almost noon and Tanya babysat a glass of Merlot. The kids would be home from school in a few hours. She closed her eyes, took a deep breath, and took another swig of wine. She dismissed the nagging feeling that crept upon her. The typed betrayal resting against the coffee maker taunted her. Tanya poured another glass of Merlot, she went over to the envelope and turned it away from her.

"I will do this, "Tanya coached herself, gulping down the burgundy fluid.

Chapter Three

Bitterness Knows Her Name

Tanya despised herself for having children. She never wanted children; but her estranged husband always talked about wanting children. She continued to take birth control until Grayson found out. When he threatened divorce for her deception, Tanya promised to stop taking the pills and they could try to get pregnant.

fffff

They met during high school. A slender and very attractive girl at five-feet-eight inches, Tanya seemed the ideal catch. She had many suitors but wasn't interested in dating an average guy. She was determined to become a famous fashion designer. Tanya had goals and refused to allow anything or anyone to get in the way of her goals. Then she met Grayson, the tall, dark and very handsome, Grayson Roberts.

Grayson came from an upper-middle class family that demanded excellence in academics, work, and friends. Although family life was demanding, when Grayson met Tanya he knew she would be his wife. His fellow classmates warned him that Tanya was a hard case; but Grayson wanted her and nothing would get in his way. One day during lunch, he introduced himself to Tanya.

"Hi, my name is Grayson, and yours is?" Grayson asked, extending his hand.

"Hi," Tanya replied, not looking up from her drawing pad as she ate lunch.

Grayson withdrew his hand and sat down next to her.

"So, what are you drawing?" He asked, leaning over her shoulder.

Her flow of creativity was being interrupted, which irritated her, and Tanya angrily glanced over at Grayson.

"Did I ask you to have a seat?" She hissed.

"Whoa, Nelly! I'm just trying to be friendly. What's your problem?" Grayson retorted, regaining his composure. "I'm sorry to sound a bit irritated; but I'm not used to unfriendliness."

"I don't know what you want; but as you can see, I'm trying to get my work done for art class," Tanya said, rolling her eyes.

"I didn't mean any harm. Really, I didn't. You draw pretty well. What is that you're drawing?" He asked.

"I'm in fashion designing and have to draw a few outfits for my final, which is due tomorrow. I apologize if I sound nasty; but I am very serious about perfection. I hope you understand," Tanya shared, returning to drawing.

"I understand. Can we talk another time when you aren't so busy?"

"I don't know. Maybe. I really need to get back to

my project, okay?"

"Sure thing. Catch you later."

As he got up to leave, Tanya turned and asked, "Who are you anyway?"

"My name is Grayson," He responded.

"I know your name; but who are you?" Tanya asked again, suspiciously.

"I'm just a guy trying to be friendly. That's all," He returned. "Have a good day."

fffff

Life wasn't easy for Tanya. The oldest of ten, five girls and five boys, she had to make her own way and take care of her siblings. Foraging for food was her main task and greatest feat. As much as she hated it, Tanya knew she could not let her brothers and sisters starve. Their parents worked but spent most of their money on parties and gambling. Tanya went to the local grocer and asked shoppers if she could push their shopping carts to their cars for a few dollars. Although it was against store policy, the manager, Mr. Johnson, knew of the Morrison children's situation and allowed

Tanya to solicit patron services. He would sometimes give her a loaf of bread, a gallon of milk, cereal, and luncheon meat. Tanya was ashamed to receive charity; but she and her siblings had to eat.

Her parents married very young, at eighteen and sixteen, and seemed less responsible than their ten children. Tanya loved her parents; but she has a deep-seated hatred for them for them, too. She couldn't recall when that hatred began; but it grew deeper each day as Tanya hustled to feed her brothers and sisters. From the time Tanya was two years old, there were screaming newborns almost every year for eight years. Her parents fought constantly and all Tanya knew was daily arguments, hunger, and insecurity.

Why her parents stayed together was a mystery to Tanya. She figured it must be better to have them both than to have just one parent with a lot of crying kids. Tanya despised her life and would do almost anything to get out of that hellhole.

fffff

Fashion had been Tanya's passion since she was a

small child, before starting kindergarten. She noticed the women at Mr. Johnson's grocery store all decked out in the finest and latest fashions. She would run home, grab her school note pad and sketch her favorite outfit she had seen that day. Soon Tanya realized her pictures were very good. Her Art teacher at Rogers Elementary entered Tanya's award-winning artwork in an annual art exposition and contest, which confirmed her talent.

"Wow, Tanya. That's very good artwork," Ms. Brown said, looking over Tanya's shoulder.

"Thank you, Ms. Brown. Someday I'm going to be a famous designer. You wait and see," Tanya stated confidently, coloring a picture of a formal, red gown.

"I'm sure you are going to be the best the fashion industry has ever known. Keep up the good work," Ms. Brown encouraged, patting Tanya's shoulder and walking over to a student seated behind Tanya.

Ms. Brown's encouragement was all Tanya needed. Just a little reassurance that she could be the best fashion designer the world would ever know was the drive she needed. Nothing was going to stop her.

She had to get out of that lousy house with all those screaming kids. Most of all, Tanya didn't want to feel hunger pains ever again. Additionally, she was determined to never have children – NEVER!

fffff

The thought of having children made Tanya cringe. She saw how her mother had babies but never nurtured nor cared for them. Tanya couldn't remember the last time her mother told her or her siblings she loved them. Her father told his kids he loved them but only when he was drunk. He would pull Tanya close and through whiskey soured breath he would tell her, "You're my first born child. I love you." The smell of his liquor breath made her sick to Tanya stomach; but at least he said he loved her.

Tanya's late grandmother, Grandma James, often stopped by, fussing at her daughter, Tanya's mother. She would nag her for not taking better care of her children. Grandma James constantly reminded Tanya's mother what a horrible mother she was. She would walk through the apartment, picking up dirty diapers, soured milk bottles, and wiping the snot-nosed grandchildren.

Ms. Morrison would shrug off the chiding and tell her mother that if she cared so much, why she didn't take the kids. That snide remark always infuriated Grandma James and led to loud arguments between the women. Mr. Morrison usually left as soon as Grandma James entered to avoid her criticism.

When the shouting match between grandmother and mother reached a high pitch, Grandma James would leave but not before calling Mr. Morrison a gambling deadbeat and drunken fool.

fffff

Crying babies, dirty diapers, and snotty noses were just too much for her to consider as a lifelong goal. Tanya was having none of it.

Those episodes and her poor home life were influential in Tanya's decision to remain childless. She couldn't understand who in their right mind would want such a responsibility or live like her parents. Tanya was sure she didn't want their lives and would do anything to avoid having children.

    "Who needs that mess," she thought to herself, scribbling away on her notepad. *"I'm going to be famous and the world will know my name for sure."*

Chapter Four

For the Love of Money

Grayson loved Tanya; but he refused to take her abuse much longer. He knew she needed help, he could see Samantha and Tavis were suffering greatly. What kind of man was he to walk out on his wife and children, leaving his children with such an unstable, angry person? Grayson tried to justify his cowardly actions by convincing himself that leaving was the best for everyone. Nevertheless, he could not shake the fact that Tanya's goal was to punish his children because she never wanted children; but mostly because they looked so much like him. As afraid of becoming a single parent, Grayson decided he would take his children. He loved them more than life; and he could learn to be a better parent with the help of his parents.

The night Grayson came home from another late evening at work, Tanya sat at the dining room table sipping a glass of red wine. He knew when Tanya drank it was going to be a very colorful and eventful evening.

"Where the hell have you been?" Tanya jeered. "And don't tell me you've been working late again, you lying ass!"

Letting out a deep sigh, Grayson slipped off his shoes at the front door, and cautiously walked over to Tanya, attempting to kiss her on the cheek. Tanya jerked away avoiding his kiss.

"Don't start. You know I've been working late this week. My caseload is very heavy this month," Grayson explained. "I showed you my list of active cases, remember?"

Grayson realized nothing he said would suffice because Tanya was always angry, especially since giving birth to Samantha and Tavis. Lately, her anger worsened. She often punished him, blaming him for talking her into getting pregnant. Tanya's frequent outbursts worried Grayson more than before. It seemed she literally hated him; but Grayson loved Tanya with all his heart. He wanted to make her life better; and that's why he became a corporate attorney. He knew she needed professional help. He chalked Tanya's nasty behavior to possible depression and begged her to seek help.

"For God's sake, Tanya, I'm begging you to get some help. I think you're depressed," Grayson pleaded. You haven't been right since you had Samantha; and it's gotten worse after Tavis' birth."

"I don't need a shrink! I didn't and still don't want to be a mother!" Tanya snapped, slamming the wine glass on the end table, shattering it into pieces.

"I've watched your emotional decline and it's terrifying and painful. The most painful part is you refuse to bond with Samantha and Tavis. You ignore them. You always scream at them. You need help.

Tanya glared at Grayson and slowly rose from her chair, heading toward the kitchen. Nervous, Grayson carefully watched her retrieve a broom and dustpan from the pantry. Returning to the shattered wine glass, Tanya dusted its remnants from atop the end table and swept up the remaining chards on the surrounding floor into the dustpan. She did not respond to Grayson's concerns.

"I called our family doctor and made you an appointment for next Wednesday at one o'clock p.m.," Grayson shared. "Since I'll be out of town for a few days, I made it for next week because I want to be there for you."

Returning to the kitchen to dump the broken glass, Tanya rejoined Grayson in the living room.

"Sure, Grayson, if you think that's best," Tanya replied, not meaning a word.

"Thank you, Baby. This is for the best. I just want our family to be happy; and you deserve happiness, too," Grayson, said pulling Tanya into his chest and kissing the top of her head.

Grayson disappeared up the staircase, leaving Tanya sitting by the glowing, crackling fireplace. Rubbing her hands together over the open flames, Tanya thought, *"That's right, Grayson. I'll be right here waiting for you to take me to see some quack."* Laughing into the fire, Tanya silently planned her revenge.

fffff

Grayson worked long hours for his corporate clients. His six-figure income provided a beautiful, big home for his small family. He bought Tanya the best cars, appliances, clothing--anything she asked for. He even paid for her annual trip to fashion week in Paris, France. Yet, it seemed nothing he did satisfied Tanya. When he came home from a long day's work, he would summon Samantha and Tavis to the family room and ask them about their day. Tanya hated it when he did that. She didn't want the children to get any of his attention. Grayson would often cut his time with Samantha and Tavis to

accommodate Tanya's envy. There were no rewards
to his actions and consolations; and it was wearing
him down.

"Tanya, we need to talk," Grayson said, sitting
in the chair next to Tanya.

"So, you want to talk about why you work late
all the time leaving me here with those damn kids all
day?" Tanya huffed.

"Come on, Tanya. Samantha and Tavis are the
sweetest kids I know. How can you call your babies
"those damn kids"? You know they can hear you,"
Grayson said sorrowfully.

"You can call them what you want. I told you I
didn't want any kids; but you had to have kids. I told
you that if I had them you would have to raise them.
I wanted more for myself. I should be a famous
fashion designer by now. You promised me the
world. You promised me I could do anything I
wanted if I gave you kids. Now, look at me. I'm
sitting in this lonely ass house being mommy to kids I
never wanted!" Tanya shouted, slamming down her

red wine, splashing the dark, red liquid across the table.

"I'm sorry, Tanya. I told you I would get a nanny if you wanted. You refused because you didn't want another woman in your house. What am I to do, give my babies away? All I want is for you to be happy. I work hard and long hours so I can give you whatever you ask; but that isn't good enough. What do you want from me?" Grayson asked, frustrated.

"What I want is peace and a fashion career. I don't want children! I never did! Can you make them go away? If not, then you are useless!" Tanya scoffed, pushing her chair away from the table to leave.

As Tanya began to rise, Grayson grabbed her arm and pulled her close to his face.

"I have stood by and listened to you bitch, moan, and groan about being a mother to our two beautiful children. I have watched as Samantha breaks her neck to please you, to get you to say you love her. I have stood by and watched as you refused to hold her, or Tavis, after their births. You won't look at your own children or tell them you love them, Tanya! What kind of mother would refuse love to her children? I have had enough of your crap! I have spent the last fifteen years bending over backwards to give you a good life; yet, you constantly begrudge my hard work. If you think you're tired, then you don't know how tired I am!" Grayson screamed, pushing Tanya until she stumbled backward.

Tanya was shocked. Grayson had never raised his voice to her during the twenty years they have known each other. Even when she was at her meanest, Grayson maintained his composure. That characteristic was what made him a well sought after corporate attorney. His calm demeanor won many cases for his law firm; and clients adored him. Grayson wasn't perfect; but family meant everything to him. He came from a very close family and enjoyed being a father to Samantha and Tavis. Grayson could not understand why Tanya couldn't love their children. What happened to her that made her so bitter about motherhood? She never talked about her family. She never visited her hometown. Grayson knew to avoid mentioning those forbidden topics if he didn't want an infamous Tanya-scathing-tongue-lashing.

As Grayson prepared to leave the dining room, Tanya took a deep breath.

"Once again, you walk away like a punk! Grow some balls!" She cursed with wine-baited breath.

fffff

Her words stung Grayson to the core. What hurt the most were the faces staring at him from the top of the spiral staircase. This had to stop. Samantha and Tavis deserved a better life. Grayson knew he had to make plans to separate from Tanya and get the kids into a more stable environment. His parents were willing to take the children for a while until Grayson could get his affairs in order. Although a corporate attorney, Grayson knew the best divorce attorneys in the industry. It wasn't difficult getting a legal separation. The problem would be Tanya. He knew she wasn't going to go away easily. She always liked to fight; and Grayson knew he needed to prepare for the nastiest fight of his life.

fffff

Tanya disliked Grayson's parents and, especially, his sister, Carol. She was envious of their relationship and lifestyle. His parents loved him and warned him about Tanya's attitude when they began dating in high school; but Grayson knew the good side of Tanya. He knew she wasn't always pleasant; but when she was, life was so good. He believed that once his parents and sister got to know Tanya, they would love her, too.

Mr. and Ms. Roberts loved Grayson so much and wanted the very best for him. He was a scholar athlete and decided to forgo a football scholarship for an academic scholarship at Yale. Tanya was also very smart receiving a 4.0 GPA upon high school graduation. Traphagen School of Design in New York offered her a full scholarship. Life was looking good for Grayson and Tanya.

Grayson admired Tanya's tenacity and focus. She had a determination for success that he envied. Tanya pushed Grayson to succeed in all his high school courses and football. Her push for his success seemed excessive; and sometimes Mr. Roberts was suspicious of her motivation. Yet, Grayson would always come to Tanya's defense. He shared how difficult her life was at home and how she only wanted the best for him.

"I guess that's okay as long as she isn't pregnant," Ms. Grayson would say, half-joking and half-serious.

His sister, Carol, thought Tanya was a mean wench and very controlling. She never understood how Tanya got her talons into her brother. Grayson was six-feet-four, built like an Adonis, brilliant, and he had such a kind and gentle spirit. Tanya was as venomous as a cobra. She was the complete opposite of Grayson. When it came to Tanya, Carol rarely held her tongue.

"I don't know what you see in that tart," Carol

quipped. "For a beautiful girl, she has the nastiest attitude. I cannot stand her!"

"Come on, Carol. Give Tanya a break. If you knew her family dynamic, you wouldn't be so hard to judge her," Grayson replied, kissing Carol's cheek.

"I guess, but she had better treat you right or I'll kick her scrawny ass," Carol joked.

"Carol! Watch your mouth," Ms. Roberts declared.

"Sorry, Mom," Carol laughed, leaving for the kitchen. "I'll go wash my mouth out with vanilla bean ice cream."

Chapter Five

The Cloak of Darkness

Samantha was an emotional wreck. She heard her brother cry for the very last time. It was time she did something more to protect Tavis from Ms. Essie's brutal anger. Today would be different. Samantha summoned up the courage and headed toward the living room to stand up to Ms. Essie and tell her where to go.

"I have to do something or Tavvy will die. I just know it!" Samantha whispered under her breath.

What brought on this newfound courage was

what happened to Tavis that cold February day. Samantha returned from school to the sounds of whimpering coming from a nearby coat closet. Although faint, she could tell it was Tavis.

"Tavvy, is that you?" Samantha called out. The only response was more whimpering.

"Who the hell is that?" A familiar, angry voice shouted out from the living room. "I said who the hell is that?" Ms. Essie demanded.

Samantha froze in her steps. She didn't know whether to answer or head toward the whimpering sound. Suddenly, the sound of creaking floorboards shook her out of her daze and she answered, "It's me, Samantha."

"You little fool! The next time I ask *who the hell is that* you had better answer me quick. You hear me?" Ms. Essie scathed.

"Yes, Ma'am," Samantha replied, hoping Ms. Essie wouldn't come into the hallway. Her wish came true when the creaking noises stopped and Samantha could hear the air in the plastic covered sofa squeeze out like a slow, long and airy fart.

Samantha turned her attention to the muffled sounds escaping the coat closet. She was horrified knowing how dark it must be inside that small, cramped room. She slowly crept to the door. The closer she got the clearer Tavis' cries became. What could she do? What would she do? Samantha knew she was risking a major beating if she opened that door. Ms. Essie was cruel and evil. She would stop at nothing to break every bone in Samantha's body. She seemed to get joy out of watching Samantha and Tavis cry, whimper, and shake from each beating. Ms. Essie was a sadist and found great joy in laying all three hundred pounds of fleshy power against the fragile bodies of the children. Samantha had to think quickly. She had to save her baby brother.

"Tavvy, please don't cry," Samantha whispered assuredly through the closet door. "I know you're scared; but I need to figure out how to get you out, okay?"

Through tears, Tavis responded, "Ok, Sam. Ok,

I'll be good. I promise."

"You're a very good boy, Tavvy. I am so proud
of you for being so brave. I'll be back. I promise,"
Samantha said, slowly backing away from the door
and heading to the living room.

fffff

Ms. Essie sat in her usual spot, in front of the
TV watching her soaps. With an orange soda,
chocolate donuts, and a cigarette, she was a force to
be reckoned with. Her stare could almost kill a
grown man. Her eyes seemed black to Samantha, as
black as her rotten soul. Samantha wanted to hate
Ms. Essie; but the more evil she inflicted on her and
Tavis, the more pity Samantha felt for her.

"What a sad woman she must be," Samantha
said under her breath.

"What did you say, you little heffa?" Ms. Essie
retorted. "You got something to say to me? If you
do, it better be good or I'm going to kick your ass."

Samantha didn't know how to respond. She
knew she had to do something to rescue Tavis from

that dark abyss.

"Ms. Essie, where is Tavis?" Samantha asked after a few seconds.

Samantha could see the muscles and veins pop out in Ms. Essie's tightened neck. That usually happened when a beating was about to happen. If a beating was in order, Samantha knew she would have to take it if Tavis' release from hell was going to happen.

"What did you say to me, girl? I know you didn't just ask me where is Tavis? Who the hell do you think you are, his mama?" Ms. Essie growled, getting up from her plastic covered sofa. Samantha stood frozen. She didn't know what was going to happen next; but it wasn't going to be good. What had she done? Had she caused more pain for Tavis? What was Ms. Essie going to do to her? To Tavis? Before she could think another thought, Samantha felt a sharp pain on the left side of her face. There was a sudden and horrific pain in her lower back. She felt sick and almost vomited. Then, she heard Tavis' blood curdling screams.

"What have I done . . .," Samantha said before collapsing and hitting the floor face first.

Chapter Six

Too Much Trouble

Tavis sat in horror as he listened to Ms. Essie beat his big sister. "Save me! Save me! Save me!" He repeated softly to himself. "I'm just a little boy. I'm just a little boy. I'm just . . ." Before Tavis could finish his sentence, the door swung open with force. "You little bastard! Get up right now!" Ms. Essie screamed, almost yanking Tavis' right arm out its socket.

Tavis knew better than to cry out; but the pain was more than his twenty-pound body could bear.

Ms. Essie dragged him past his sister lying in a pool of wetness. Tavis didn't know if it was blood or pee. It didn't matter, Samantha was hurt and she wasn't moving.

"Samanthaaaaa . . ." Tavis cried out.

"Shut the hell up! That little bitch deserves every beating she gets from me. You're next!" Ms. Essie promised.

"Please, Ms. Essie. I'll be good. I promise. I promise!" Tavis pleaded to no avail. Ms. Essie slung his small body against the hallway wall. Before reaching the floor, Tavis' little four-year-old body went limp.

"I hate those damn kids," Ms. Essie spewed, kicking Samantha's motionless body and plopping down on her plastic cover sofa to finish watching her soaps. "That will teach those half-breeds to interrupt my damn soaps."

fffff

Tavis regained consciousness to find Samantha still motionless. He crawled to her side, wrapped his arms around her waist and promised to be good.

"Sam, I'm sorry. I promise to be good. I promise!" He whispered in her ear.

Tavis needed his big sister and wanted to help her; but he didn't know how. All he could do was lie closer to her hoping that would help. But Samantha didn't stir. Blood continued to trickle from her mouth into the pool of liquid that consisted of blood and bile. The forceful kick from Ms. Essie ruptured Samantha's intestines and badly bruised her kidneys. Samantha was in serious trouble and there was no one to help.

"Don't leave me here, Sam. She's gonna hurt me some more," Tavis cried, hugging Samantha's waist tighter.

The floorboards began to creak, and the vibration of heavy footsteps drew closer.

"Girl, get your ass up! Get up right now or I'll kick you again!" Ms. Essie shouted at Samantha's motionless body.

There wasn't a stir coming from the little girl balled up in a fetal position. Tavis held his sister's waist tighter praying she would move. Nothing. Not a sound. Not a twitch. Tavis began to cry uncontrollably.

"Get off her, boy!" Ms. Essie demanded, rolling Samantha's body over with her elephant-fat foot.

Watery nastiness covered Samantha's bruised body. Her mouth slightly opened revealing two missing front teeth with coagulated blood pasted to the side of her mouth. Her swollen face was unrecognizable from the hard fall. Tavis was horrified.

"Sam, wake up. Stop sleeping, Sam. You have to wake up," He cried, flinging his arms around her blood-soaked neck.

"I said move out the way!" Ms. Essie shouted, kicking Tavis in the side causing him to buckle and cower to a nearby corner.

Rocking in the corner and wrapping his arms around his legs pulled to his chest, Tavis began to think about his father.

"Daddy, why did you leave us? Mommy

doesn't love us. Ms. Essie doesn't love us. Her sons are mean to us. Daddy, why did you leave us?" Tavis asked underneath his breath, rocking faster and faster and faster. "Oh, God, please tell my daddy to come get us. Tell him I promise to be good so he can love us again. Oh, God, please!"

Chapter Seven

I Want What I Want

Samantha and Tavis were finally asleep. Tanya could not believe Grayson was choosing those brats over her.

"I gave you fifteen years of my life and this is how you repay me by leaving me for the kids I never wanted? We'll see about that," Tanya snorted, plotting how she could hurt Grayson.

Tanya was beside herself with anger and self-loathing. She could not believe she had compromised her dreams for children. There was nothing wrong with having children as long as it wasn't her having them. Tanya loved Grayson. He was her world. He was tall, handsome, very smart, charismatic, and from a wealthy family. Although Mr. and Ms. Roberts had objected to their relationship, particularly because Tanya was Black, Grayson's parents would do anything for their son's happiness. They knew Grayson was a good son, but very stubborn. Moreover, Tanya had Grayson wrapped around her little finger. This was the main reason Tanya secretly laughed because Grayson's parents knew they couldn't win. The only problem standing in Tanya's way was his sister, Carol.

Carol loathed Tanya and the feeling was mutual. Carol knew Tanya wasn't good for her little brother; but she also knew Grayson deeply loved Tanya. Whenever Tanya would come for dinner, Carol made sure she had other plans or work. She was a very successful news anchor and would plan after hours meetings or attend events so she wouldn't have to lie to her parents and Grayson.

Tanya didn't care. All she wanted was Grayson's full attention; and she got it. This was very troubling to Mr. and Ms. Roberts; but more so for Carol. She had watched her little brother excel in everything he touched; but when it came to Tanya, Grayson seemed to lose his way. During their senior year, Grayson's grades began to falter, which alarmed his parents, coaches, and teachers. His scholarships were at risk; and Carol wasn't about to allow some tramp scamp to ruin her brother's dreams.

One morning as Carol sat in the kitchen having a cup of coffee, the doorbell rang. She took another sip, got up and headed to the door. As she approached, it rang again.

"Hold on, I'm coming!" Carol announced loudly, increasing her pace.

When she reached the door, Carol looked through the side window. To her dismay, it was Tanya. Carol's face expressed her disdain and disappointment. Tanya just tilted her head and smirked. Taking a deep breath, looking down and back up, Carol unlocked the front door.

"Good morning, Tanya," Carol greeted dryly.

"Good morning, Carol," Tanya responded, glaring at Carol. "Grayson is expecting me for breakfast. May I come in?"

Before Carol could respond, Tanya pushed herself past Carol and headed toward the kitchen.

"Oh, come on in, Tanya. We're having breakfast in the kitchen," Carol mockingly shouted, rolling her eyes. "I cannot STAND that woman!"

fffff

Carol was no bigot; but she really didn't like Tanya's ghetto, hard attitude. At five-feet-eight inches, Tanya was gorgeous and her size was quite intimidating. She had a fantastic sense of style and commanded the attention of everyone when she entered a room. However, once she opened her mouth, Tanya's arrogant attitude was a turnoff.

Carol was also very attractive. Although petite, Carol was a powerhouse at KTKC-4. She had always wanted to be in journalism; and as kids, she and

Grayson would act as co-anchors while sitting at the breakfast table. Sometimes their parents would pretend to be the camera crew following Carol around as she reported on the latest action of her stuffed animals and their pet dog, Moxie. She had superb broadcasting talent and Carol was very good at investigative reporting. She had warned Grayson she would have Tanya investigated because there was something very suspicious about anyone who didn't want her boyfriend or his family to know about, let alone meet, her family.

"Carol, please just let it go. You don't know what Tanya's been through. Her life has been very hard," Grayson pleaded.

"Grayson, I wouldn't feel this way if Tanya wasn't such a tart! She is rude to Mom and Dad, and she talks to you as if you are a dog. I won't stand by and allow her to continually disrespect our family this way," Carol threatened.

"I'll talk to her. There are reasons for her behavior. I know that's no excuse; but give me a chance to handle this, okay?" Grayson asked, softly caressing the top of Carol's left hand.

"I love you, Grayson, and I only want what's best for you. That's the least you deserve. Mom and Dad are sad because they know you deserve so much better; and they can see Tanya is manipulating you," Carol continued, raising her right eyebrow and exhaling a long sigh.

"I'm not trying to hurt anyone, Carol. I want to make everyone happy; but I also want to be happy. Can't you understand that?"

Carol didn't respond. She knew her brother had a giving heart; but was naïve about females, especially Tanya's type. Carol knew Tanya's type very well because Carol didn't make it to the top of her news career by being a pushover. Grayson fell in love easily; and she spent many nights comforting him from heartbreak. Carol was determined to protect her little brother; and if Tanya stepped out of line, the fledgling fashion designer would regret it. She had friends in high places; and Carol could put a serious damper on Tanya's career.

fffff

Ms. Roberts placed fresh, squeezed orange juice on the table. She took her normal seat at the opposite end of the breakfast table her husband's empty chair.

"Grayson tells us you have been accepted on a full scholarship to Traphagen School of Design in New York. That's very impressive, Tanya," Ms. Grayson complimented, placing a cloth napkin on her lap and smiling at Tanya.

"Yes, Ma'am. I'm not surprised. I've worked very hard all my life. I deserve the very best," Tanya shamelessly boasted.

"Tanya, what do your parents think of you going to New York?" Carol asked, pouring herself a glass of orange juice.

Carol knew this would upset Tanya and she didn't care. Tanya was such an arrogant piece of work; and Carol would take a dig every chance she could get. Tanya made it very easy.

"Carol!" Ms. Roberts said, surprised at Carol's

rudeness.

"It's a legitimate question, Mother. You would want to know if Grayson and I were accepted to such a prestigious school. I'm sure Tanya doesn't mind me asking, right Tanya?" Carol smarted, looking at Tanya over the rim of her orange juice glass.

Tanya wasn't amused. She was seething; but maintained her composure. She wasn't about to let Carol one-up her. If she wanted to play this game, Tanya was more than happy to oblige.

"Of course, my parents know about my scholarship and are very happy for me. I will be the first in my family to attend college. My parents are very proud of my accomplishments," Tanya lied, coldly staring at Carol.

"That's wonderful, Tanya. I'm so happy for you. You are very talented; and I know you will be very successful as a fashion designer," Ms. Grayson responded, trying to extinguish the catfight.

"Where is Grayson? Why hasn't he come down for breakfast?" Tanya asked.

"I'm sorry, but Grayson had to meet his guidance counselor at the high school. They needed to complete his scholarship package. He and Mr. Roberts left about an hour before you arrived," Carol gladly shared.

Tanya had her glass of juice to her mouth when her face became expressionless. With hands shaking, she returned the glass to the table spilling some.

"Is everything all-right, Tanya?" Ms. Roberts asked.

"Sure. Everything's fine. It's just Grayson invited me to breakfast and he isn't here. I find that to be very rude," Tanya replied, obviously upset.

"He didn't know about the appointment until this morning. The advisor called to tell Grayson a deadline had been overlooked and that they needed to get the application completed and mailed before the post office closed today," Ms. Roberts explained.

"I see," Tanya whispered through clinched teeth.

fffff

When Tanya found out Grayson had been accepted to Yale and didn't accept the scholarship to New York University, she was very upset. She wanted him near her while she attended Traphagen. How dare he not want to be near her? Tanya didn't want Grayson out of her grasp, so when he showed her the scholarship paperwork, Tanya removed the deadline notice and shredded it. If Grayson missed the scholarship deadline, he would have to make other plans; and Tanya would convince him to attend New York University. It wouldn't happen as she planned. Grayson would be in Connecticut and she in New York. She had to step up her game, so Grayson would be hers permanently. The only way that would happen was through marriage; and Grayson's parents and his bitchy sister, Carol, weren't about to have that right now.

Faking pregnancy wasn't Tanya's thing; but if she had to, then so be it. All she had to do was pretend for as long as possible, and then fake a miscarriage. That would seal Grayson's loyalty. He was big on family and responsibility. Tanya would have Grayson by all means necessary; and if faking a pregnancy was the way to get him, she would do it.

"Tanya, are you okay?" Ms. Roberts asked.

"Huh?" Tanya asked, snapping out of her daydream.

"Is everything okay? You look a bit ill," Ms. Roberts said with concern on her face.

"I am feeling a bit under the weather. I need to go home and lie down. Tell Grayson I will call him later," Tanya said pushing away from the breakfast table.

"I hope it wasn't something I said," Carol added with a smirk.

Tanya ignored Carol's snide remark, and quickly left before Carol or Ms. Roberts could say good-bye.

"I sure hope she is okay. She didn't look so good, Carol," Ms. Roberts said as she finished her scrambled eggs and wheat toast.

"I'm sure she'll be okay, Mother," Carol reassured wondering what that she-devil was plotting.

"I'm sure that little evil mind of hers is on full speed. I have to protect Grayson or Tanya will destroy him," Carol thought to herself, sipping the last of her coffee.

fffff

Carol had found a piece of the letterhead of the scholarship application on the floor near the shredder in their father's office. She knew Grayson wouldn't do such a thing and immediately, her thoughts turned to Tanya.

"That little bitch! She's trying to destroy my brother's dreams. I'll call Miss Jensen at the high school and get this taken care of before it's too late. Then, I'll deal with Miss Sabotage. Tanya will regret ever knowing Grayson," Carol thought plotting her revenge.

What Carol, or her parents, hadn't anticipated was the ace Tanya had up her sleeve. They wouldn't

be able to pry Grayson from her controlling claws.
She knew she already had an emotional grip on
Grayson; but those claws were about to get tighter
around his heart. To seal the deal was the
announcement of a baby. She didn't care if she never
wanted children. Tanya wanted Grayson, his prestige,
and a way out of the projects; and Carol wouldn't
intimidate her. Additionally, Tanya found pleasure in
pissing her off.

fffff

Grayson always talked about having a house
full of kids; and Tanya told him she didn't want
children, especially since she had to help raise nine
brothers and sisters. She didn't want anything to do
with parenthood. When Grayson found out she had
no desire for children, he broke up with her. He told
Tanya it was important for him to have a family and
only wanted to marry someone who wanted a family,
too.

Tanya didn't want nor could she afford to lose
Grayson. He was her escape from her awful family

life. She loathed the idea of having children. They were too much work. She just didn't want to be tied down to all that responsibility. Her parents didn't seem to let ten children slow them down. They just dumped them on Tanya. This wouldn't be her fate. She could fake wanting children; and when they married, she would stay on birth control. She hoped eventually, Grayson would think he was sterile. Then, they could would live happily ever after childless.

fffff

Sometimes the plans people make succumb to the will of nature. Tanya would soon find out that plotting for evil and selfish reasons can turn as quickly as a tornado, be just as deadly, and decimate both innocents and the guilty in its path.

Tanya awoke with a massive headache. She had suffered migraines before, but nothing like this. She sat up on the edge of the bed holding her head in her hands. Grayson was still asleep when she gathered enough strength to make it to the bathroom to retrieve her migraine medicine.

It had been seven months since Grayson and Tanya has returned from their honeymoon in Greece. For two weeks, they stayed in a Peloponnese villa overlooking spectacular scenery and gorgeous sandy beaches. They visited the Archaeological Museum and toward Pylos to see the remains of the palace of Nestor. The breathtaking beauty of Epidaurus' Greek amphitheaters, the Byzantine castles and ruins in Monemvasia and Methoni enamored Tanya. She had suggested they move to Greece; but Grayson didn't like the idea. He wanted to be near his parents and Carol. Family was everything to him.

When they returned to the States, Grayson surprised Tanya with the keys to a beautiful, fully furnished, three-bedroom home. Grayson took great care to learn Tanya's tastes and worked with an interior designer to have the home decorated and furnished while he and Tanya were on their honeymoon.

When Grayson carried Tanya over the threshold, she let out a gasp. At first, he thought she was disappointed. To his surprise, Tanya turned to him and kissed him long and hard.

"Baby, this — is — amazing!" Tanya said between kisses.

"I'm so happy you like it," Grayson chuckled, pretending to grab his heart as though having a heart attack. "I thought I would have to tear it down and start over."

"You are such a silly man. You knew I would love it. You got all the colors, fabric, furniture, and accessories just perfect. You're amazing."

Tanya returned, running into the living room. Grayson had out done himself. The living room looked like a palace with antique white walls trimmed in mountain sage-green and nutmeg. Oil paintings of historical Greek seaside villas, Parisian gardens, and beautiful Italian hillsides adorned the walls. A large Lebanese rug accented the nutmeg ceramic tile floors. Streams of sunlight beamed down from the vaulted ceilings and engulfed Tanya as she slowly turned around and around in awe of their gorgeous home.

As she stood under the sun's light, Tanya's beauty mesmerized Grayson. Watching her reminded him why he had fallen in love with her. It wasn't just Tanya's beauty; but her child-like excitement whenever he did nice things for her. All Grayson desired was to make his wife happy for the rest of their lives. This was a great beginning.

"Baby, I'm so glad you're happy," Grayson said, walking up behind Tanya and wrapping his arms around her waist.

"This is a dream! Thank you so much, Grayson."

"You know I'd do anything for you. I love you so much."

"I love you, too."

"We will be happy here. You are free to design until your heart is content."

Grayson turned Tanya around and kissed her passionately. Grabbing his hand, Tanya led him up the spiral staircase. She was falling in love with her new life. Grayson was falling in love with his new life and more with his new wife.

fffff

It was an exciting time for them. They were living their dreams. The previous year, Grayson joined the Schumer and Wise law firm. His legal talents made him the star rookie. There was talk of making him a partner within the next few years. This was Tanya's dream. She would be part of the society elite. She looked forward to the extravagant dinner parties, operas, ballets, and symphonies. Attending these events gave Tanya reasons to buy a new dress and accessories. Although Grayson questioned her purchases, he never asked her to stop. Even if he had, Tanya had already made up her mind she would do what she wanted.

fffff

This headache was almost more than she could stand. Swallowing two pills, Tanya sat on the side of the tub until the pain lifted. As she stood up, she became nauseous. Tanya reached for the phone and dialed her doctor's office. The nurse asked her a few questions before scheduling an appointment for the following day.

"Ms. Roberts, are you allergic to anything?"

"Not that I know of."

"Have you eaten anything that may have expired such as tuna salad with mayonnaise, undercooked meat?"

"No."

"When was your last period?"

"The fifteenth of last month."

"It's the twentieth. Are you on your period now?"

"I'm having spotting; but not a full period."

"Okay. Let's get you scheduled for 1:30 p.m. tomorrow to see Dr. Griffin. Will that work for you?"

"Sure."

"Great. We'll see you then."

Still feeling nauseous, Tanya opened the top drawer of the nightstand and retrieved her appointment book. Noting the time of her doctor's appointment, she scribbled a brief note: *I am NOT pregnant.*

Tanya's present life was very different from her life in the projects. Tanya vowed never to return to her former life. Grayson was her way out. Nothing would get in her way, not even a pregnancy.

Chapter Eight

Needle in a Haystack

Grayson was devastated. The day had come and the separation papers were prepared and ready to serve Tanya. He and Tanya had discussed the terms of the separation. He would take the children to his parents to live until he found a suitable place. Tanya could stay in the house until the judge made final property decisions. She would also have visitations as often as she wanted. Grayson promised to make the transition as smooth as possible. Tanya seemed to agree to the terms and why wouldn't she?

There would be no children to get in the way of her fashion dreams. She would have the house to live in for at least another six months and enough money to buy a new home.

What Grayson couldn't understand was the disappearance of Tanya and his children. Why would she take the kids she hated so much? He knew the answer and shivered at the thought. Tanya took the kids because she wanted Grayson; and she wouldn't let him have the kids without her. It was all about revenge.

Grayson sat in the middle of the floor in the main dining room. Tanya had left everything, even the children's clothes.

"Where could she have gone without taking anything? What is she going to do to my kids?" Grayson thought angrily, heat rising to his face.

Grayson spotted a photo of Samantha and Tavis on the fireplace mantel. He went over, picked up the picture, and burst in the deep sobs.

"God, please don't let anything happen to my

precious babies. I've tried hard to be a good father. Protect them for me until I find them. Oh, God, please!"

fffff

"Thanks for calling Robert J. McNamara Detective Agency. Sharon speaking," the friendly female voice announced.

"Hello, this is Grayson Roberts. Your agency came highly recommended. I need immediate assistance locating my children," Grayson blurted. As one of the top corporate attorneys in Kansas City, Grayson was legendary for his calm demeanor. However, he quickly lost control of his emotions as he shared his story with the telephone stranger.

"Mr. . . . Mr. Roberts. Please calm down and slow down," Sharon interrupted. "I understand your urgency; but we must first get you in here. When can you stop by?"

"Can I come by today? I have to get this matter handled with urgency," Grayson replied, regaining his composure.

"Let me check Mr. McNamara's schedule. Please hold."

Grayson's heart raced. It had been almost six months since Tanya left with Samantha and Tavis. He contacted everyone—her parents, her girlfriends, and extended family. They claimed that they hadn't heard from Tanya. Her parents seemed genuinely surprised and hurt by the news. Grayson's parents and sister were also hurt, angered, and horrified. Where could they be? The voice from the receiver shook Grayson from his thoughts.

"Mr. McNamara said he can see you at five-thirty this evening. Will that work for you, Mr. Roberts?" Sharon asked.

"Of course it will!" Grayson replied with excitement. "Thank you for your help and tell Mr. McNamara I'm so grateful he can see me on such short notice."

"No problem, Mr. Roberts. Bring any information that will help us in your case like recent photos, your children's school records, social security numbers, etc. Please don't worry. We will find your children," Sharon reassured Grayson. "We'll see you at five-thirty sharp."

fffff

Grayson had never been a patient driver; but today was worse. He was anxious to get to the investigator's office and the evening traffic jam was wearing down his nerves. The slow highway traffic forced him to reflect on his marriage and family life over the past few years. He couldn't understand why marriage was so hard, especially when he gave Tanya everything she asked. He was a very good father and provider. Grayson shuddered to think that his marriage disintegrated because of the births of his children. *How could Tanya not love Samantha and Tavis? They were the best kids in the universe.*

Shaken from his daydream by the loud honking of the horn of a more impatient driver, Grayson waved in his rear-view mirror, whispered an apology at the distant figure and continued his trek to meet Mr. McNamara.

fffff

Robert McNamara was a tough and seasoned former police officer and Marine Special Ops veteran. He had seen his share of violent criminals as well as death and destruction during wartime. He went into the Marines right out of high school at seventeen and spent his twenty-three year career in Special Ops retiring as a Master Gunnery Sergeant. War changes even the hardest man; and McNamara had a reputation for being hard as titanium. His fellow Marines nicknamed him, "Titanium Mac". He could shoot and kill without flinching. Taking down the enemy was his duty and McNamara took his military responsibilities very seriously. During his career, he received every military honor available. His fellow Marines lived to die for him; and McNamara lived to die for them.

However, Titanium Mac had a very strange but special gift. He could get the enemy to talk without torture. McNamara's superiors were amazed how enemy combatants became instantly relaxed when he entered their holding area. McNamara recognized this special talent as a child. Even in kindergarten, all the kids wanted to be his friend and throughout his elementary through high school education, he was never without a mob of friends. Although his exterior seemed rough and tough, people seemed to feel an instant bond with McNamara.

The Afghanistan and Iraq wars changed McNamara significantly. Killing adults was a tough task; but often times unavoidable. The end for McNamara began with a particular incident in the fall of 2001. While on a reconnaissance mission with his team, they received orders to flush out known Taliban operatives in the village of Kandahar. The Special Ops team was to execute fatal strikes within fifty meters of the village. Although that was a very close perimeter, McNamara's team was trained well.

Earlier, Kandahar was buzzing with activity. Villagers seemed to go about their normal routines of goat herding, women shopping in at the open market, kids running and playing, and old men sitting around smoking pipes and cigarettes. The Marines knew this activity was most likely a disguise because the Taliban were known to use elderly, women, and children in an attempt to fool their enemies. They would often times use them as human shields. But, McNamara felt something was different about this scene. He didn't feel right about this mission.

McNamara pulled his captain aside and shared his concerns. He requested the captain recheck their intelligence. Trusting McNamara and knowing his stellar reputation, the captain radioed the command to report their location, what they found, and to reconfirm the intelligence. The command assured the team the intelligence was correct and confirmed by several sources.

As night fell, and McNamara's team was in striking position, his Captain received orders to strike the village. Immediately, the Marines began their deadly assault on the Taliban-infested locale. After ten minutes of launching bunker busters, throwing AN-M14 incendiary hand grenades through windows, kicking in doors and riddling the interiors with hundreds of Colt 9mm SMG rounds, the village fell silent. The evening air was thick with smoke with homes and other shelters ablaze.

Donning gas masks, McNamara's team stealthily and methodically cleared each location. When no bodies were found McNamara breathed a sigh of relief. As the team began to retreat and the captain had reported the outcome, he thought he heard something coming from a nearby burning structure. He put his right forefinger to his lips motioning to his captain and fellow marines to be quiet. McNamara focused his attention to where he thought he heard the sound. Over the crackling of burning and falling structures, the team heard the muffled screams of women and children.

Carefully, but rushing toward the screams, the team made their way to the burning structure. It appeared to be a small storage facility made of wood and mortar. With guns loaded and pointing toward the building, McNamara was the first to kick in the door. Smoke poured out of the door forcing McNamara back onto the dirt road. To his horror, he could make out the faces of elderly men, women, and children huddled together as the flames began to engulf them. McNamara's eyes locked with the eyes of what appeared to be a little girl. Her eyes pleaded for him to rescue her from the deadly inferno. He attempted to burst through the flames again, but another Marine tackled him and dragged him to safety. All he and the other Marines could do was watch as the screaming souls disappeared behind the flames. McNamara's eyes never left the screaming eyes of the little, burning Afghani girl. Her face would haunt him for eternity.

The intelligence had been wrong; and McNamara had been right. He had never betrayed his intuition. That is what kept McNamara and his team alive. His team was still alive; but innocent men, women, and children were dead — burned alive. Those pleading and screaming eyes invaded McNamara's every thought. How would he, or how could he, reconcile with those terrified and pleading eyes? He didn't believe it was possible during his lifetime.

Chapter Nine

Faded

Samantha laid still on the hospital gurney surrounded by medical staff trying to save her fragile life. Although unable to move, Samantha could hear everything going on around her. Through the pokes, prods, and sticks, all she could think about was the safety of Tavis.

"God, please keep Tavvy safe. I'm sorry I let him down. I tried to protect him. Protect him, please, God. I tried to be a good big sister," Samantha thought.

"Code blue!" A nurse shouted, pressing on Samantha's chest. "Get the crash cart. We're losing her!"

Samantha heard the beeping of machines, adults shouting words she couldn't understand, and she felt the painful pressure on her chest from the up and down pushing. She knew something was wrong and wanted to tell the doctors not to worry; but no sounds escaped her lips. A cold chill settled in Samantha's bones. It felt as though everything around her was fading. As her thoughts turned to her little brother, one lone tear rolled down her right cheek. A nurse standing nearby wiped the lone tear away with a tissue and caressed her forehead. Samantha felt the softness of the cloth and the nurse's touch. She was thankful to feel cared for.

All Samantha wanted was to have a family filled with love and laughter. She missed the days when her daddy would come home from work and play with her and Tavvy for hours. The sound of her daddy's laugh made everything right in her and

Tavvy's world. God had to be somewhere out there. She had never asked for much. Maybe this time God would hear her plea.

"And, God, could you tell my Daddy that Tavvy and I are sorry for being bad kids. We didn't mean to be bad. We tried hard to be good. We didn't mean to make him mad and leave us," Samantha thought as the heart monitor beeped loudly and erratically. Suddenly, the monitor lines went flat.

fffff

Every night, the pleading eyes of the burning Afghani girl awoke McNamara. The recurring nightmare began soon after he and the Special Ops team returned to their base camp. There was the routine debriefing. An intelligence team conducted the debriefing and when the captain informed them of the burning Afghani civilians, the Special Ops team was reminded those civilians were just collateral damage.

"That's the hazards of war," a senior intelligence officer explained without emotion. "You

Marines were trained to deal with this type of incident and you did an outstanding job."

". . .and you did an outstanding job . . . and you did an outstanding job . . . and you did an outstanding . . .,"the burning Afghani girl repeated over and over, her flame-filled eyes piercing McNamara's soul.

McNamara quickly sat up in bed, sweat dripping from his naked torso. His pajama pants were soaked as well. He had the same nightmare every night. A daily feast on a gallon of Vodka and two Ambien couldn't drown the nightmare. It seemed to slither its way through McNamara's intoxicated brain cells.

It had been over a year since the Kandahar incident; but McNamara's PTSD had engulfed his life. Intelligence had informed McNamara's team that they later discovered that the day of the incident, the Taliban had kidnapped all elderly, women, and children from a nearby village. Updated intelligence reports were not received until the next day. McNamara knew protocol. The military would never admit fault, especially when civilian casualties were involved.

In February 2002, Master Gunnery Sergeant, Robert "Titanium Mac" McNamara was honorably discharged from the United States Marine Corps. For his dedicated service, he received two Purple Hearts for his Kandahar mission. When he left his retirement ceremony, McNamara held the Purple Hearts in his hands and considered throwing them into a nearby dumpster. However, he quickly reconsidered and was determined to use them as painful reminders of the burning and pleading Afghani girl. In her memory, he vowed to rescue as many children, especially little girls from those who hurt them. This would be his life's mission.

fffff

Grayson paced the floor of his office. An hour earlier, the private investigator left him a message requesting an urgent meeting. Grayson was in a weekly staff meeting when his secretary handed him a note and quickly excused himself. The investigator insisted he deliver the news in-person.

If he has bad news, I don't know what I'll do. I hope nothing has happened to Samantha or Tavis. Grayson's mind began to race. He reached for the crystal water pitcher on the mahogany sofa table. He began to pour himself a glass of water when it suddenly slipped from his hand shattering on the marble floor.

"Mr. Roberts, is everything okay?" His assistant chirped through the phone's intercom.

"Yes, I'm fine. A glass just slipped. Could you please call housekeeping to come clean this up?" Grayson reassured, closing his eyes and taking a deep breath to calm his nerves.

"Sure, Mr. Roberts," The intercom voice replied.

Grayson was on edge. He couldn't understand why the investigator would not tell him what he had found over the phone. All he could do was to wait anxiously for another thirty minutes; and that thirty minutes seemed like a lifetime.

fffff

"I understand your schedule is very busy, Mr.

Roberts; but I would not have held off sharing what I found if it wasn't critical to do so in person," McNamara explained, settling in the brown, leather chair across from Grayson.

"Yes, I'm a very busy man but not too busy to find my children," Grayson responded, a bit irritated. "Just tell me what you've found."

McNamara began rubbing his mustache with his right index finger and thumb. Looking at Grayson with concern and sadness in his eyes, he cleared his throat.

"Samantha is in ICU at General Hospital," McNamara reported.

McNamara watched as all the color left Grayson's face. Believing Grayson would pass out; McNamara leaped to his feet, grabbing Grayson by the shoulders. He led Grayson to the sofa, and gently sat him down.

"Take a deep breath, man. It's going to be all-right," McNamara reassured Grayson, returning to his seat. "Your daughter was badly injured. I don't have all the details; but I can assure you she has been stabilized."

Grayson's head was spinning. He couldn't believe what he was hearing. He began to feel a bitter anger arise within him. Trying not to scream, Grayson put his hands to his mouth and closed his eyes. After several minutes, he regained his composure.

"Who gave you this information?" Grayson asked, taking a sip of lemon water.

"A fellow Marine works at General Hospital an attending physician. During our weekly card game, he was telling us about this little girl who was found by a nurse outside the ER," McNamara shared, trying hard not to make the story sound so cold.

Leaning back onto the sofa and placing his left elbow on top of some pillows, Grayson held the left side of his forehead between his left thumb and index finger. He was in a daze. His baby had been brutally hurt. Who could have done such a cruel thing to his sweet baby?

"Did Tanya finally snap?" Grayson spoke into

the air.

"Do you think your wife did this?"

"Huh?" Grayson asked confused by the news. "No! I didn't mean . . . I have to get to the hospital and get my baby," Grayson told McNamara as he reached for his coat and keys.

"That may be a problem, Grayson," McNamara responded. "My friend told me the authorities and social services are investigating. I would strongly recommend you taking an attorney with you."

McNamara was right. Grayson knew he needed to keep his head and contact his friend, Maxwell, who was one of the best defense and family law attorneys in the state.

"Thank you, McNamara. I appreciate everything you've done," Grayson said, standing and extending his hand. "I'll need the file as well. The balance owed will be in your account by tomorrow."

"No problem, Grayson. I'm very sorry for delivering this sad news; but now you know where to start."

McNamara shook Grayson's hand, grabbed his hat and coat. Before leaving, he turned and looked somberly at Grayson.

"Again, I'm so sorry. I've delivered bad news before; but never about a child. This tears me up inside. If I can be of further assistance, don't hesitate to call me."

With his coat thrown over his right arm, McNamara put on his hat, and left.

Staring at his closed office door, Grayson wished it would open into a world where everything in his marriage and children were safe and happy. He could hear the playful laughter of Samantha telling Tavis to stop tickling her feet. She had the most infectious laugh, which hovered in the vaulted ceilings. Her blue eyes seemed to look into his soul. Samantha had that effect on her daddy. At that thought, Grayson slipped back down onto the sofa and wept.

Chapter Ten

Maddening Contemplation

Pacing the floor in the women's restroom of the President Hotel in downtown Kansas City, Tanya couldn't believe the trouble she had gotten herself into. With little money and her promise not to reveal the underground organization's location or its leadership, She felt trapped. She knew she had to do something about Samantha's disappearance; but how would the organization handle her admission to such a disastrous mistake? They would surely deny any association with her. There were no signed documents or records indicating the organization participated in hiding Tanya and the kids. She was on her own.

With Tavis sitting quietly on the antique grey divan, Tanya rubbed her eyes, walked over to the porcelain sink and splashed cold water on her face.

"Okay. Think, Tanya, think," Tanya said to herself in the mirror. "You've really screwed up. How are you going to get yourself out of this mess?"

fffff

Grayson stared through the glass of his little girl's ICU room. As a nurse busied herself checking Samantha's vitals, fluid levels, repositioning her body, and injecting some type of medication into her IV line, Grayson thought about Tanya and Tavis. He couldn't understand how his family had disintegrated to this horrible scene.

"Mr. Roberts," a station nurse called out, "You have a call. She says it's urgent."

Taking a deep breath, Grayson slowly walked over to the nurses' station. *"It's probably Mom or*

Carol," He thought.

"Grayson speaking," He announced into the receiver. There was no response; but Grayson could hear someone breathing. "Hello? Who is this? I don't have time for games!"

"Grayson, this is Tanya."

Grayson quickly covered the receiver and asked the nurse if there was somewhere he could get privacy. The nurse pointed to an empty conference room adjacent to the family waiting area. She put the call on hold as Grayson hurried to the conference room.

Without saying a word, Grayson picked up the call and listened. He was fiercely angry with Tanya. She had all but destroyed his family. He had tolerated her bad attitude, selfishness, and poor motherly relationship. Now, he was at the hospital watching his little girl being kept alive by machines. What could she say to calm his bitter anger.

"Grayson, are you there?" Tanya asked, voice quivering.

"Yes, I'm here, Tanya," Grayson responded.

"I know I messed up badly. I need. . ."

Before Tanya could finish Grayson interrupted.

"You're damned right you messed up badly!" He shouted into the phone. "Our little girl is lying in a coma in ICU. What were you thinking taking my babies away from me? What the hell happened?"

"Oh my god," Tanya sobbed. "I promise I had nothing to do with hurting Samantha. I promise!"

"You had everything to do with this," Grayson blared into the receiver, but quickly quieting down so the detectives couldn't hear. "You took my kids and left without cause. You didn't even want them. You did this to spite me."

Grayson listened as Tanya sobbed deeply through the line. For the first time since they married, she showed emotion. When he proposed, bought her a huge house, cars, diamonds, trips around the world, Tanya had never shed a tear. Even when her father died, she didn't cry. Hearing her sob was confusing and seemed to quiet Grayson's anger. Yet, he was still suspicious. Was she crying because of this situation that would most likely cause her legal problems or was she emotional because she really loved Samantha and felt remorse?

"Where are you? Is Tavis with you?" Grayson asked, more calmly this time.

"He's sitting here on my lap."

"Is he okay? Where are you? I want to pick you and Tavis up."

"Tavis is fine. We're at the downtown President Hotel."

"Okay. I'll be there within the hour. I must warn you. They have stationed a police officer outside Samantha's room and social services have been here throughout the day. You may be charged with abuse and neglect or worse."

"I don't care anymore. I'm exhausted and want to come home," Tanya answered, sobbing deeply again.

"I will handle the legal issues. I just want you and Tavis here with Samantha and me. I'll see you in the lobby within the hour."

"Thank you, Grayson. By the way, I want you to know I've been thinking about everything. I realize I have serious issues to work out; and I'm willing to get help."

"We'll talk about that later. Let's just get you and Tavis home."

Hanging up the phone, Grayson sat down, tears freely flowing. He hadn't cried this much since his beloved grandfather died when Grayson was a senior in high school. His six months of emotional hell was ending. In an hour, he would be reunited with his family. Although his parents and Carol would have major issues with Tanya returning, they were the least of his worries. He could handle their reactions. All he wanted was his family back together no matter what it took or how much it cost.

Retrieving tissue from its container on a side table in the conference room, Grayson wiped his face. He reached into his left, black blazer pocket, retrieved McNamara's business card, and called him with the news. Grayson agreed to let him drive. McNamara thought this was the best idea since Grayson hadn't slept in several days. Additionally, he wanted to ensure the authorities did not tail them. If so, he knew how to lose them.

fffff

"McNamara, I really appreciate this," Grayson said, resting in the passenger seat of McNamara's 1963, Mercury Comet convertible.

"No problem. You didn't need to take this drive alone."

"I know you were working on finding Tanya and Tavis; and I will pay you in full."

"Hey, man. Don't worry about it. Focus on getting your family back together. We'll deal with the money matters later," McNamara replied, patting Grayson on the shoulder.

"Can I ask you a personal question?" Grayson asked, staring out the passenger window, his breath fogging up the glass.

"It depends on the question."

Grayson turned toward his new friend and studied his face. Being an attorney had its advantages; but Grayson had a supernatural gift of accurately reading people, well, most people.

"Do you have a family?"

"Nope," McNamara replied, staring straight ahead.

"May I ask why not?"

"Sure you can ask; but I don't know if I want to answer."

"I'm sorry for intruding. I'm not wearing my attorney's hat, but my friend hat."

"I know, Grayson. I appreciate it, too. I haven't talked about my private life with anyone except my Special Ops buddies," McNamara said, quickly glancing over at Grayson.

"Do you have a family, children?"

"No family or children."

"Have you ever wanted a family?"

"I don't know how to answer that one, except my lifestyle doesn't have room for intimacy."

McNamara griped the steering wheel tightly, his knuckles turning white. Grayson took that as a clue to end the inquiry.

"Thanks for allowing me to ask such personal questions, McNamara."

"No problem. Now, let's focus on getting your wife and son back home."

The men returned their attention to their windows, quietly continuing their drive to the President Hotel.

Chapter Eleven

Strange but Familiar Connection

Samantha laid still on the hospital gurney surrounded by medical staff trying to save her fragile life. Although unable to move, Samantha could hear everything going on around her. Through the pokes, prods, and sticks, all she wanted to do was scream that she was okay.

There was that familiar voice again. Samantha focused on that voice. It soothed her. She felt deeply connected with its deep, yet gentle tone. Why couldn't she remember its owner? Samantha was troubled about this revelation. The only person she could remember was her brother, Tavis. She saw only his face in her dreams. Who were their parents? Samantha knew something was wrong because every child had parents. Why couldn't she remember her parents?

Grayson continued to whisper in her ear. "My baby, I'm so sorry," He repeated through heavy sobs.

Samantha felt drops of warm wetness slowly trickle down her right cheek. She didn't know whether it was her tears or the voice's tears. The spiritual connection she felt was overwhelming. Samantha was determined to recognize the voice's owner.

"You don't have to worry anymore, Daddy's home."

Daddy? Samantha thought. Maybe if she could see his face she would remember him.

I'm here! Can you hear me? Samantha screamed internally. She didn't know she was in a coma and no one could hear her screams. *I need to see his face. I want to remember!*

Grayson kissed Samantha's forehead and caressed her cheeks. "You will awake soon; and I promise I will find out who did this to you," He reassured. "I will never let you or Tavis out of my sight again."

"Daddy!" Although confused, Samantha felt a bond with the voice. All she needed was to see its face.

fffff

"Ms. Roberts, you are under arrest for child neglect, child abuse, child abandonment, and first degree battery," The older detective said, as the younger detective handcuffed Tanya. "You have the right to remain silent . . ."

In shock, the surreal activities left Tanya speechless and shaking. McNamara rushed to Samantha's bedside to tell Grayson what was happening. Grayson ran out just in time to see the detectives on both sides of Tanya as the elevator doors closed behind them.

"Don't worry, Baby! I'll have you out tonight," Grayson shouted into the closed elevator doors, pressing his forehead against the cold metal.

McNamara walked over to Grayson and placed his hand on his shoulder. "Let's call your parents so they can take care of Tavis; and I'll drive you to the station," McNamara suggested. "I have friends on the force. Don't worry. We'll have her out in no time."

Turning around, Grayson slid down onto the gray-speckled linoleum floor. He looked up into the fluorescent-lit ceiling and sighed deeply.

"McNamara, I'm a smart man. I love my family so much," Grayson shared. "I just don't understand what's happening."

McNamara walked over to Grayson's right side and slid down beside him.

"Grayson, being smart has absolutely nothing to do with experiencing life," McNamara said. "It's not the time to self-blame. We need to find out who did this and get justice."

"You're right. I need to keep it together for

Samantha and Tavis' sakes. My family knows I love them; and I will show them how much by finding who hurt my baby girl. They will regret living when I'm done with them."

For the first time since seeing his battered daughter, Grayson felt a deep, burning rage. It was a foreign emotion and it scared him. It was a vengeful anger; and he didn't want to ignore it. He would keep his thoughts sacred because he knew his parents, Carol, and McNamara would talk him out of revenge.

"No problem, McNamara. Let's take care of business."

After calling Grayson's parent, McNamara rejoined Grayson and Tavis at Samantha's bedside.

"Your parents will be here shortly," McNamara reported.

"Thanks, again for all your help," responded kissing the top of Tavis' head and gripping Samantha's hand.

fffff

Grayson picked up Tavis, kissed him and

handed him to his mother. He hugged his parents before he and McNamara headed to the police station. He could hear Tavis' soft whimpers. Grayson turned back, rushed over to his father who was holding Tavis, and grabbed Tavis.

"Tavis, don't worry. I'm never leaving you again. Daddy has to take care of a few things; and I promise I'll be with you at Pawpaw's and Grammy's tonight, okay?"

"Okay."

Giving Tavis a last kiss and handing him back to his father, Grayson disappeared down the hallway with McNamara. Tavis' eyes fixed on where his daddy disappeared and was scared he would never see his father again.

fffff

Hugging his grandfather's neck tightly, Tavis' grandparents walked into Samantha's room. Their aunt Carol sat next to Samantha, holding her hand and caressing her cheek. Mr. Roberts lowered Tavis so he could kiss Samantha goodnight.

"Good night, my beautiful angel," Mrs. Roberts said softly in Samantha's ear and kissed her forehead. Mr. Roberts did the same. Carol kissed her hand. Before leaving, Tavis told his grandfather he forgot to tell Samantha something very important.

Leaning in closely, Tavis whispered quietly into her ear, "Daddy's home." Then, he, his grandparents and Aunt Carol left for the evening.

"Tavis!" Samantha shouted in vein from her comatose prison. Her eyes fluttered several times, and then stopped.

The nurse checking her vitals had her back to Samantha and hadn't noticed the movement. She noted Samantha's vitals on the chart and left. In her darkness, Samantha fought the will to give up. The pain was terrible and the nurse didn't know the pain medicine wasn't working. It didn't matter. Samantha was determined to return. Their daddy was back. Most of all, Ms. Essie needed to be stopped.

About the Author

Clarissa Burton has been writing poetry and short stories since age 8. She has published articles in the Charleston Post-Courier, the Kansas City Star, Flourish Magazine, and the Kansas City Small Business Monthly. She publishes blogs on several online websites. She has written a book of poetry, Travel-A Poetry Compilation, two children's books, Elijah's Great Race and Princess Onyx Precious Gems, and a family tree booklet, The Black Family Tree.

Clarissa has a B.A. in Psychology from Ottawa University – Overland Park, Kansas, and a Master's in Business from Webster University – Kansas City. She served honorably in the U.S. Navy from 1984 to 1990. She is the mother of three adult children and grandmother. She currently lives in the Midwest with her tuxedo cat named, Bootsie.

For more information about Clarissa Burton, upcoming events, or to schedule a reading, visit www.queenofthepenbooks.com.

More Books by Clarissa Burton

POETRY

Travel – A Poetry Compilation

Travel – The Journey Continues (Release Date: November 29, 2013)

CHILDREN'S

Elijah's Great Race

Princess Onyx™ Precious Gems

Micah's Grumpy Day (Release Date: September 2, 2013)

SELF-HELP

The Black Family Tree®

Upcoming Releases in the Faces Novel Series

Daddy's Home

Darkest Before Dawn

Small Packages

Self

Captured

For more information, visit

www.queenofthepenbooks.com

www.ingramcontent.com/pod-product-compliance
Lightning Source LLC
Chambersburg PA
CBHW071312130626
46556CB00004B/1585